SPARTAN &
The Green Egg

— THE POACHERS OF TIGER MOUNTAIN —

Nabila Khashoggi

ILLUSTRATED BY MANUEL CADAG

BOOK 4

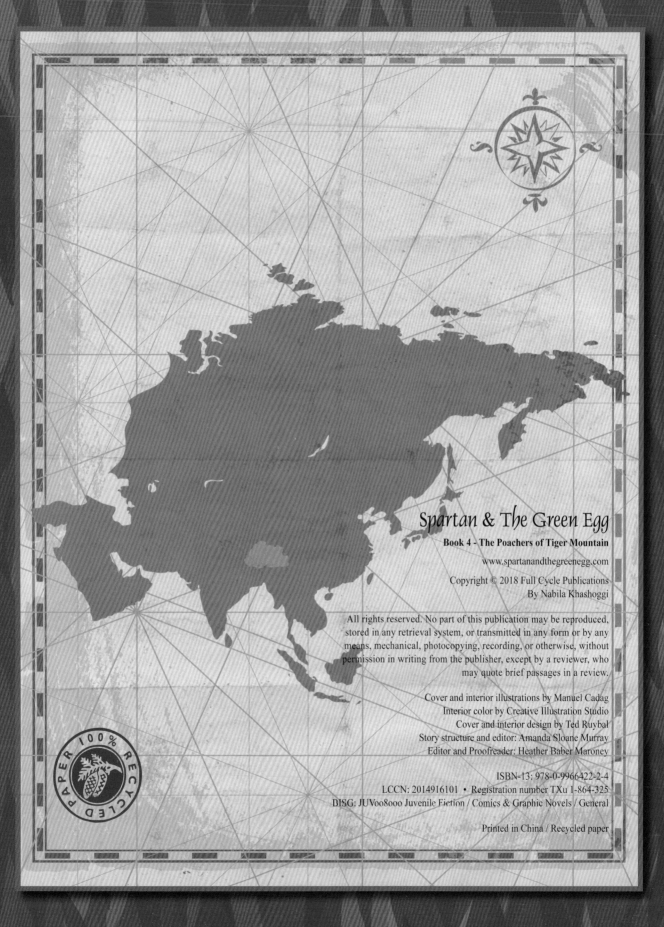

Spartan & The Green Egg

Book 4 - The Poachers of Tiger Mountain

www.spartanandthegreenegg.com

Copyright © 2018 Full Cycle Publications
By Nabila Khashoggi

Cover and interior illustrations by Manuel Cadag
Interior color by Creative Illustration Studio
Cover and interior design by Ted Ruybal
Story structure and editor: Amanda Sloane Murray
Editor and Proofreader: Heather Baber Maroney

ISBN-13: 978-0-9966422-2-4
LCCN: 2014916101 • Registration number TXu 1-864-325
BISG: JUV008000 Juvenile Fiction / Comics & Graphic Novels / General

Printed in China / Recycled paper

Spartan & The Green Egg®

Full Cycle PUBLICATIONS

Quality reading and entertainment

www.fullcyclepublications.com

P. O. Box 57005, Murray, Utah 84157
Tel: 1 (801) 299-2705 • Fax: 1 (801) 905-3348 • Email: info@fullcyclepublications.com

Part of the proceeds of the sale of this book go to
The Children for Peace ONLUS. www.thechildrenforpeace.org

To Baba,
Our Greatest Adventurer.

2

The landscape suddenly uprooted and began to move around them.
It seemed like everything was flying.

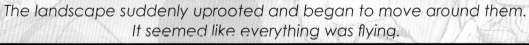

Grimm leaped up and began running in circles.

Max found his data screen monocle. He can access information about anything instantly. This special device was a gift from Egg.

Katie's gift from Egg was her magic sketchpad and crayons which can bring a picture to life. Katie made sure the sketchpad was in her backpack.

Tor had yet to receive a gift tailored to his talents.

Where's my something special?

Be patient, Tor. I know you will receive something cool when the time is right.

The kids adjusted their headpieces and left the spaceship.

Spartan took an unsure step, then stopped.

I don't want to get us lost.

Grimm sees something!

Grimm's eyes were fixed as he pressed against Spartan.

A large cat, snow-white with black spots, emerged from the trees, cocked its head and considered them.

Max immediately checked his monocle.

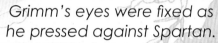

It's a snow leopard. They're endangered and incredibly rare.

Grimm, wait!

As they fought through the snow, it was clear they didn't have a chance.

The leopard was quick and nimble as it raced through the trees, and Grimm stayed close on its tail.

He looked down and saw that his boots were sending vibrations all the way up and down his legs.

Spartan was about to despair, but then he noticed his feet getting strangely warm.

All they could do was hold on as they caught up to, then PASSED, a confused Grimm.

Spartan saw the edge of a cliff approaching, and braced himself on his heels.

They all stopped JUST in time to keep from plummeting over the edge.

AHHH!

SCREEEEECCH

His boots screeched to a halt.

Meanwhile, the leopard effortlessly leaped from rock to rock all the way down the sheer cliff face.

When the leopard reached the bottom, it looked up at them, and then disappeared into the undergrowth.

Well, that was exhausting!

What now?

We go there.

That village? It looks remote and vacant . . .

. . . and beautiful!

23

The town square was filled with hundreds of people. Their attention was focused on a group of archers.

It's some kind of tournament.

THWANG!

It wasn't a very reasonable explanation, but nobody seemed to mind as they all enjoyed the delicious food.

I think I've eaten enough for a week!

We're going to teach you how to shoot an arrow.

THUD PLIK!

After the archery lesson, everyone gathered to watch a play performed by the villagers.

What's this play about?

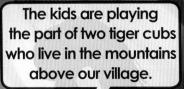

The kids are playing the part of two tiger cubs who live in the mountains above our village.

What happened to them?

We believe the poachers destroyed the cubs' parents. We haven't seen them in months.

Yay!

The "cubs" chased the hunters around in circles. The crowd cheered.

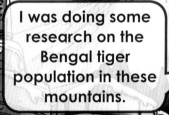

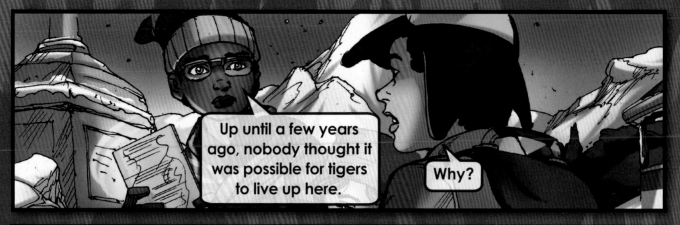

Up until a few years ago, nobody thought it was possible for tigers to live up here.

Why?

High altitude, extreme weather and a limited food source—but there are a few special places where tigers have been found. I guess this is one of them?

Well, until the terrible poachers get them all!

Yes, Bengal tigers are endangered, but it might not be too late.

If we could get the tiger cubs to Tiger Mountain, then they'd be safe. Where is it?

You deserve this, Tor.

Thanks!

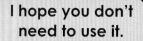

I hope you don't need to use it.

Good luck.

41

Red dots began to appear on the map one at a time.

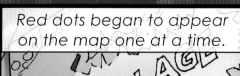

Village . . . that's where we are . . .

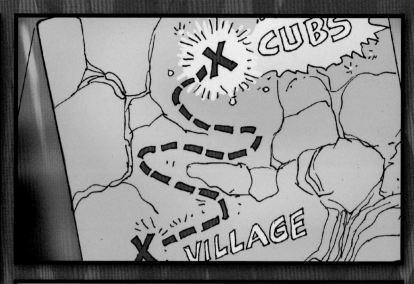

That's where we'll find the tigers . . .

The dots continued crossing over several mountains, arriving at a third X. This one was marked . . .

Tiger Mountain! We have a plan!

The map spun rapidly, shrinking in size . . .

POP

Thanks, Egg.

. . . and tucked itself neatly into Spartan's backpack.

They climbed higher and higher up the mountain. As they did, the forest became sparser, the land rockier. They felt a bit lightheaded.

We are very high up on this mountain.

Katie, are you okay?

Yeah. Just . . . catching my breath. I'm finding it a bit hard to breathe.

Grrr..

What is it, Grimm?

Is something behind me?

Errr . . .

Suddenly, a creature sprang out of the woods towards them. It was brilliant orange—with black stripes—

Yikes!

And it was moving incredibly fast!

Baring his sharp teeth, the tiger cub jumped up towards Katie.
Grimm leaped up to knock Katie out of the way.

The tiger cub was suddenly in a giant bubble floating gently to the ground.

52

What's the Tibetan word for brave?

Let me check. It's "Pawo."

Nice to meet you, Pawo.

Hours later, Spartan and his friends found themselves on an ever-narrowing path as it wound around the face of the mountain.

They followed Pawo, who had no problems picking his way through the snow, rocks and trees. The kids, meanwhile, struggled not to trip and fall.

Pawo seemed to know where he was going, and kept a quick pace.

As he quickened to match Pawo's pace, Max tripped on a fallen tree branch.

KRACK!

He fell to his knees— then his eyes widened.

Max realized he was looking directly over the edge of a cliff that dropped down into a deep gully. He backed up slowly.

Oh, man! Be careful, everyone! It's a long way down.

You worry about yourself, clumsy pants. We're just fi . . .

Whooooa!

Katie's words were cut off as the rocks beneath her crumbled.
She began to fall forward over the cliff's edge.

Grimm leaped forward . . .

. . . and caught the cuff of her sleeve.

60

Everyone watched breathlessly as the female tiger cub approached.

Katie sat frozen as the cub came face to face with her.

The cub yawned, revealing long, sharp teeth.

Suddenly and unexpectedly, the cub leaned in and licked the green goo off Katie's arm with her rough pink tongue.

'The Endless Gorge'— that doesn't sound good at all.

We'll deal with it when we get there. Let's get moving. We don't have a minute to lose.

Uh—I think there's a problem. Pawo and Jigme seem to be having way too much fun to know it's time to go.

I'm not going to tell them!

Grimm likes to chase tennis balls.

I think he hears someone coming. The poachers must be back.

Wait! I've got an idea.

YES! Draw a bridge for us to use!

Thing is—I'm no engineer. I can draw a bridge, but I don't know if it will be able to hold us.

I can help with that! I love bridges. I always have wanted to build one.

Tor confidently began to instruct Katie on how to draw a safe bridge.

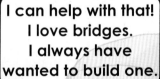

67

Spartan watched admiringly. In his own way, Tor had saved them twice. He was proving to be a valuable team member.

Here we go!

The drawing of the bridge sprang from the page. It hurled itself off the side of the gorge, launching high in the air. It landed on either side of the gorge with a loud clatter.

Suddenly, a rustling sound came from behind them.

The kids, Grimm and the tiger cubs pounded across the narrow, shaky bridge. It swayed back and forth dangerously, but held.

The poachers struggled to pull out their rifles and aim.

Spartan was the last one to cross the bridge.

Egg! Jam those guns!

WHAT IS HAPPENING!?

After them!

HURRY, SPARTAN!

Egg, make the bridge disappear! NOW!

Spartan raced across the bridge as fast as he could.

The poachers quickly stepped back off the bridge to avoid falling into the gorge.

Gesturing angrily, they yelled at the kids.

I don't need a translator to know those guys are really mad!

We made it. I can't believe it!

We can't stop now. If we're up here on the mountain after dark, then there's no telling what might happen.

Besides, it's freezing!

Egg, please blast a hole in this fence.

You got it!

BOOOM!

The metal wires of the fence shrunk away creating a large hole. Pawo and Jigme bounded through, and then the hole in the fence repaired itself.

The cubs ran up to the other tigers, sniffing and pawing.

A large adult tiger gave each cub a lick on the face.

I guess our job is done. Are we ready to go home?

The sun set behind the tall, jagged mountain peaks. The stars began to dot the evening sky.

Egg suddenly appeared and . . .

. . . grew, transforming into the big oval ship that would take them back home.

Spartan gave the cold, glittering Himalayas one last look.